A Christopher Ranch Story

Elephant Garlic
Halloween

– Written by –
Ken Christopher

– Illustrated by –
Danny Voight

– Designed by –
Articulate Solutions, Inc.

Today is a very momentous day—a time for animals of all kinds to use their imaginations.

4

This spookiest of days has finally arrived, King Lion is throwing a party, and all of Gilroy has been invited.

The Little Elephant peered through his window, so excited the day was finally here.

He couldn't wait to be his
favorite hero, and share tricks-
and-treats with all his friends!

"I've been preparing for all of the year,
and can finally say... Captain Garlic is here!"

8

"Trick-or-treat Mr. Mouse, I love what you've done:
a supremely good mummy, all wrapped up for fun."

10

"Trick-or-treat Mr. Rabbit with your magical wand.
Cast a spell for us, and then I'll move on!"

"Trick-or-treat Mrs. Bear—with your pointy hat,
you became a witch, just like that."

15

Despite all this fun, and his friends all there,
the Elephant realized something was amiss.

A new elephant neighbor has moved to town.
But on this Halloween, she wore a frown.

"What's wrong fellow elephant, what could it be?"

"Monsters and ghosts keep frightening me."

"Any time I get scared, I know what to do.
   You keep this secret, and I'll share it with you.
   Elephant garlic, known through the land,
   is monster repellant…I've got some on hand!"

"Wow! Elephant garlic just for me?
I'll be the bravest one, oh gee!"

The two little elephants went trunk to trunk,
parading their garlic for all to see.

"Trick-or-treat Mr. Monkey, I met a new friend!
She's sweet but she's nervous, though it's just pretend."

24

"Oh you elephants, everyone knows
that Halloween and costumes are just how it goes."

A spookier Halloween has never been had, and as they
shed their ghostly costumes, all nerves were calmed.

Though not quite ready for a disguise, our new elephant friend
at last had the courage to join in all the fun.

And towards the end of the night, all the animals made one last stop.

King Lion appeared and offered
a toast to their new brave friend:

"You've done it, you've done it, you've faced your fears.
The best Halloween we've seen in years!
It's thanks to you Little Elephant, you've helped her through.
With Elephant Garlic, she knew what to do!"

At a quarter past nine, right at bed time, the elephants snuggled away, with our new friend happy to have found her favorite food.

The End